BEAR IN THE AIR

By SUSAN MEYERS Illustrated by AMY BATES

Abrams Books for Young Readers, New York

For DYLAN AND TREVOR
—S.M.

FOR SEAN AND TEDDY
—A.B.

The illustrations in this book
were created using pencil and watercolor.

Cataloging-in-Publication Data has been
applied for and may be obtained from the Library of Congress.

ISBN 978-0-8109-8398-4

Text copyright © 2010 Susan Meyers
Illustrations copyright © 2010 Amy Bates

Book design by Chad W. Beckerman

Printed and bound in China
10 9 8 7 6 5 4 3 2 1

Abrams Books for Young Readers are available at special discounts
when purchased in quantity for premiums and promotions as
well as fundraising or educational use. Special editions can
also be created to specification. For details, contact
specialmarkets@abramsbooks.com or the address below.

ABRAMS
THE ART OF BOOKS SINCE 1949
115 West 18th Street
New York, NY 10011
www.abramsbooks.com

This is the bear that went for a ride,

Bounced from the stroller.

How Baby cried!

Mother looked everywhere, here and then there,
Had to go on without finding the bear.

This is the dog that found the bear,

Shook it and tossed it high in the air,

Carried it down to the sandy shore,
Trotted away with the ribbon it wore.

This is the wave that came rushing in,

Taking the bear for a watery spin,
Over and under and out to sea,
Far from the shore where the bear used to be.

This is the man out sailing a boat,

Who saw the bear drifting, barely afloat,
Lowered a net, but though he took care,
The net didn't hold and out slipped the bear.

This is the seal that popped up to see

What all the splashing above him could be,
Found the bear bobbing and took it to play
Deep in the ocean—then swam away.

This is the seaweed that tangled the bear,

Tying a ribbon of green in its hair.
Fish came to nibble its nose and its toes,
As up to the surface the bear slowly rose.

This is the bird that dived for the fish,

Came up with the bear in its beak. What a dish!
Flappity, flappity, up to the sky.
Never before had the bear been so high!

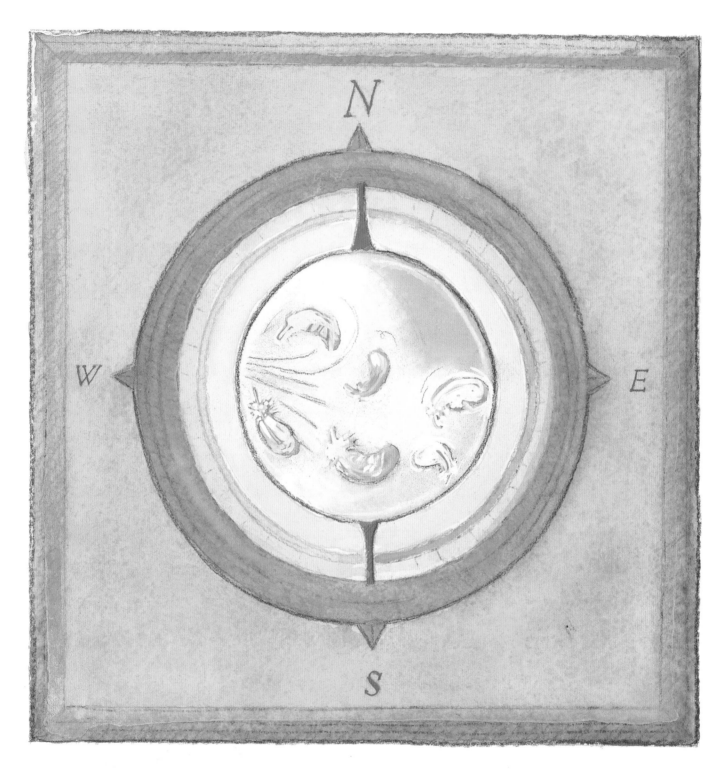

This is the breeze that made the bird sneeze,

Sent the bear tumbling head over knees,
Turning and twisting, round and around,
Bumping and bouncing back to the ground.

This is the lady who picked up the bear,

Hung it to dry in the warm summer air.

Along came Baby—what a surprise!
Mother could scarcely believe her own eyes.

This is the bear that's been everywhere,

Deep in the ocean and high in the air.

Tucked in safe so it won't bounce away,
This is the bear that's come home to stay.